NIGHT NOISES
AND OTHER MOLE AND
TROLL STORIES

YEARLING BOOKS/YOUNG YEARLINGS/YEARLING CLASSICS are designed especially to entertain and enlighten young people. Patricia Reilly Giff, consultant to this series, received the bachelor's degree from Marymount College. She holds the master's degree in history from St. John's University, and a Professional Diploma in Reading from Hofstra University. She was a teacher and reading consultant for many years, and is the author of numerous books for young readers.

For a complete listing of all Yearling titles, write to
Dell Readers Service, P.O. Box 1045,
South Holland, IL 60473.

Night Noises

And Other Mole And Troll Stories

BY TONY JOHNSTON

ILLUSTRATED BY CYNDY SZEKERES

A YOUNG YEARLING BOOK

For Barbara, Jill and Margaret

Published by
Dell Publishing
a division of
Bantam Doubleday Dell Publishing Group, Inc.
666 Fifth Avenue
New York, New York 10103

"The Loose Tooth" appeared prior to the publication of this book in the February 1977 issue of *Cricket* magazine.

Text copyright © 1977 by Tony Johnston
Illustrations copyright © 1977 by Cyndy Szekeres

ISBN: 0-440-40232-8

Reprinted by arrangement with The Putnam & Grosset Group

Printed in the United States of America

October 1989

10 9 8 7 6 5 4 3 2 1

W

The Wishes

Mole was walking in a sunny place.

He saw a four-leaf clover.

He lay down and looked at it.

His forehead wrinkled. His ears wiggled too.

Troll came walking by.

"Is something wrong, Mole?" asked Troll.

"No, nothing is wrong."

"But your ears are wiggling," said Troll.

"They always wiggle when I am thinking," said Mole. "I have found a four-leaf clover. So I am thinking of four good wishes."

"That is nice," said Troll.

"May I listen to you wish?"

"Please do," said Mole.

So Troll sat down to listen.

Mole thought deeply.

Then suddenly he shouted, *"One!"*

Troll jumped.

"What happened?" asked Troll.

"I thought of a wish," said Mole.

"Oh," said Troll. "What wish?"

"I wish I had someone to make me
dandelion tea when I am sick."

"That is a good wish," said Troll.

"Thank you," said Mole.

Mole thought again.

"*Two!*" he shouted louder still.

Troll grabbed Mole.

"What *is* it?" he said.

"I wish I had someone to tell me
when my fur needs combing."

"I like that wish," said Troll.

"But do you have to wish so loud?"

"That is how my wishes come,

loud as thunder," said Mole.

A few minutes went by.

Then Mole cried out, *"Three!*

I wish I had someone to go strolling with,

in sun or snow, in weeds or flowers."

"What about in rain or shine?" asked Troll,

picking himself up.

"Yes, in rain or shine, too," said Mole.

"Thank you, Troll."

The breeze blew the clover.

The clouds moved by, making pictures.

And everything was still, except for the buzzing bees.

That reminded Mole of something.

"Four! I wish I had someone
to bring me honey sandwiches when
I am feeling sad!"

He yelled so loudly that Troll hid.

At last Mole had made all his wishes.

He was glad. He was tired of thinking.

Troll was glad, too.

He was tired of getting scared.

"You are a good wisher," said Troll.

"Thank you very much," said Mole.

"But you don't need to make wishes," said Troll.

"Why not?" asked Mole.

"You have *me*, Mole. I will make you dandelion tea when you are sick.

I will tell you when your fur needs combing.

I will bring you honey sandwiches when you

feel sad. And I will stroll with you

in sun or snow, in weeds or flowers.

I am your rain-or-shine friend."

Mole was very happy.

"You are right, Troll," said Mole.

"I don't need this four-leaf clover at all.

I will leave it for the bees."

Then Mole and Troll walked down the hill.

"Mole?" asked Troll.

"Yes, Troll?"

"May I tell you something?"

"Of course."

"Your fur needs combing," said Troll.

The Visit

Troll went to visit Mole.

They pressed leaves into books.

They made potato stamps

and stamped them on bright paper.

Then it was time to go.

"Thank you for a lovely day," said Troll.

"Now I am leaving."

Troll looked out the window.

"On second thought," he said,

"I'm staying."

"You can't stay," said Mole.

"It is my nap time."

"I can't go," said Troll. "It is raining."

"Raindrops are nice and wet

and pitter-pattery," said Mole.

"Raindrops are nice and wet, and

they will frizz my hair!" cried Troll.

"I like to be sleek and straight.

I don't like to be frizzy."

"But you live just a few drops away,"

said Mole.

"A few drops is the same as a trillion.

I won't go unless you lend me your umbrella."

"I don't have an umbrella," said Mole.

"I don't need one. I am waterproof."

Troll frowned hard. Mole thought hard.

At last he said, "Here is a paper bag.

Put it on your head and hurry home.

You will stay dry as soda crackers."

"I will not wear a paper bag," said Troll.

"I will look like a bunch of groceries."

Mole thought again.

He went to the kitchen

and brought back the dishpan.

"Here, Troll, put this on and hurry home.

Your hairy old head will be dry as sawdust."

"Fine," said Troll.

"But what about my hairy old toes?

They will be soaking.

They will frizz like anything!"

"Here's my newspaper," said Mole. "You can

have it to cover your whole hairy body."

"What if there's wind, Mole?

And the paper blows away? Then what?"

"Then you will frizz all over the place!"

cried Mole angrily.

He was tired of thinking.

He wanted to be napping.

"What time is it?" asked Mole.

"Two o'clock," said Troll.

"Oh, dear. Nap time," said Mole.

And he pushed Troll out the door.

The rain came down in slanting streaks.

Troll tried to cover himself with newspaper.

And leaves. And a big mushroom.

But the rain trickled in.

Troll frizzed. And frizzed. And frizzed.

Inside Mole was snug, but he was not happy.

He thought, "Troll is out there
getting wet and frizzy.
He might even catch a cold!"
Mole rushed outside.
"Oh, Troll," he said. "I'm sorry.
I was mean and selfish. Please come in.
What are friends for if not to keep you dry?"

"I won't come in," grumbled Troll,

with water dripping off his nose.

"I like it here."

"Please," said Mole.

"You'll catch a cold."

"There's nothing like a good cold."

"Please, please with sugar," begged Mole.

So Troll came back inside.

Mole got a big turkish towel.

He rubbed and combed.

He slicked and sleeked.

Troll was happy. He was dry.

He looked very sleek.

And he did not catch a cold.

But Mole did.

The Loose Tooth

"Mole! Mole! Mole!" cried Troll.

"What? What? *What?*" asked Mole.

"My teeth are falling out!"

"All of them?" asked Mole.

"Just one of them," said Troll.

"Please glue it back for me."

"The tooth is ready to come out," said Mole.

"Let's help it. We'll take it out

the Old Mole Family Way."

"What way is that?" asked Troll.

"Quiet, please, Troll. I am

trying to remember."

Troll was very quiet.

Mole tried hard to remember. At last he said,

"I remember. We tie one end of a string

to the tooth. We tie the other end

to the bedpost. We wait.

And the tooth will come out—pop-o!"

"That way sounds bad for trolls," said Troll.

"It sounds very hurty."

"I will sit next to you," said Mole.

"And it won't hurt a bit."

Mole tied a string to Troll's tooth.

He tied the other end to the bedpost.

He sat next to Troll. He held his hand.

They waited for the tooth to pop out.

But nothing happened.

"Hmmm," said Mole.

"The Old Mole Family Way

is not working."

Troll looked worried. Mole thought again.

"Now I remember," he said. "We tie the

string to a chair.

Then the tooth will come out—zing-o!"

Mole untied the string from the bedpost

and tied it to a chair.

He sat next to Troll. They waited.

But the tooth did not come out.

"I know!" cried Mole. "I was all mixed up.

We tie the string to the doorknob.

Then I slam the door. And the tooth

will come right out—presto!"

"Stink-o!" said Troll. "I will not do that.

That will really hurt."

"But, Troll,

that is the real Old Mole Family Way.

I promise it won't hurt."

"Promise crisscross applesauce?"

"Promise crisscross applesauce."

"All right, Mole," said Troll. "But I

am not ready. Don't slam

the door till I say 'now.'"

Mole tied the string to the doorknob.

He opened the door. He sat next to Troll.

He waited for Troll to say "now."

He waited for a long time.

"Are you ready yet?" asked Mole.

"Please don't rush me," said Troll.

So they waited some more.

A breeze came through the door.

The room got chilly.

Troll got chilly. He sneezed loudly,

"KER-SNORT!"

"Bless you," said Mole.

"Thank you," said Troll.

"That ith very nithe of you to thay."

"Thay?" cried Mole. "Let me see your tooth."

Mole looked. The tooth was gone.

"Troll?" asked Mole. "Did that hurt?"

"Not a bit," said Troll.

"What happened?"

"You sneezed your tooth out."

Troll smiled hugely in the mirror.

"That ith the New Troll Family Way," he said

"That is a good way," said Mole.

"And you are a good friend," said Troll.

"It really helped to have you next to me."

"Yes," said Mole. "That always helps a lot."

Then they went to look for the tooth.

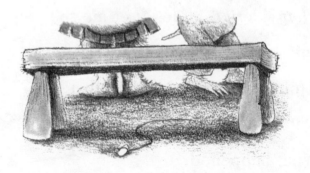

Night Noises

The night was still and quiet.

Mole lay awake, listening to the quiet.

Then he heard a hissing noise.

"Help!" he cried in a loud voice.

Troll hurried down from his house.

"Mole! Mole!" he called. "Where are you?"

"I am hiding," whispered Mole.

"Where?" whispered Troll.

"Where that hissing monster can't find me."

"But I can't find you either," said Troll.

"I am sorry, Troll, but I heard a loud,
hissing breath, and I am not coming out."

Troll listened carefully.

Hiss-pop! He heard a hissing noise.

"Mole," he said. "That is not a monster.
That is only a night noise. It's the
fire going out. Now will you come out?"

Crickle. Crackle. Rustle. Bustle.

Mole came out of hiding.

"You are right, Troll," said Mole.

"It is the fire. Now I can go back to bed."

"Good," said Troll.

And he went back upstairs.

Mole still could not sleep.

He heard a small sound in the breadbox.

"Troll!" he called.

Troll rushed downstairs.

"The monster is back," said Mole shivering.

"It is in the breadbox."

"That's a funny place for a monster,"

said Troll.

He tiptoed bravely to the box and opened it.

A tiny mouse was nibbling

on a crust of bread.

"You silly," said Troll.

"That's not a big monster."

"It isn't?"

"No. It's a small night noise."

"Oh, thank you, Troll," said Mole.

"I feel much better now. I feel like
sleeping all night long."

"Wonderful," said Troll.

"Good night, Troll."

"Good night, Mole."

Everything was quiet as quiet can be.

Then Mole heard a clack-clacking in the wind.

"Troll! Help! Save me!" he shouted.

So Troll dashed down again.

"A big, toothy monster is clacking
its big, toothy teeth outside my window,"
quivered Mole. "It is after me."

Troll listened.

"Oh, Mole, those are just friendly
night noises," he said. "They are
little branches clacking in the wind."

"You are such a good friend, Troll.
You always make me feel better."

"Good night, Mole."

"Good night, Troll. *Really* good night."

Mole crawled in bed and fell fast asleep.

Troll crawled in bed and was wide awake.

Frogs cricked and croaked in the trees.

An owl hooted. Fireflies hummed.

A wolf howled at the moon.

Troll raced downstairs.

"Mole!" he shouted. "Monsters.

Lots of them.

They are cricking and croaking

and hooting and humming

and howling too. I am scared!"

"Oh, Troll, those are just

friendly night noises."

"How do you know that, Mole?"

"A good friend told me."

"What good friend?" asked Troll.

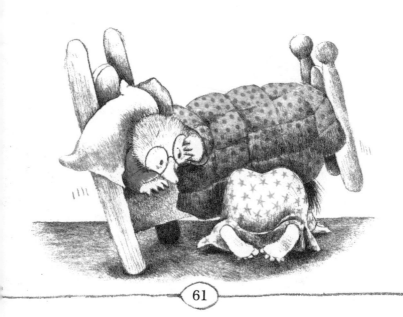

"Troll," said Mole.

"He knows a lot about night noises."

Then Mole and Troll laughed out loud.

"Mole?" asked Troll. "May I stay

here tonight?"

"That would be very nice," said Mole.

So Mole and Troll went to bed.

They snuggled down. And they felt good,

listening to the night noises

with each other.